Little Erik of Sweden

Madeline Brandeis

Edition : Culturea (Hérault, 34)
Contact : infos@culturea.fr
Print in Germany by Books on Demand
Design and layout : Derek Murphy
Layout : Reedsy (https://reedsy.com/)
ISBN : 9791041848980
Légal deposit : August 2023

LITTLE ERIK OF SWEDEN

CHAPTER I

THE GNOME

Erik sang as he skated across the lake. The lake glistened with chill, bluish crispness like steel.

It was as natural for Erik to sing as it was for most little boys to breathe. Sometimes it seemed that he had the throat of a bird.

"Down the mountainside came thundering,

Fierce and wild, a giant tall."

It was Greta who had taught Erik these fairy-tale songs. Greta made them up. She was the eighteen-year-old daughter of Fru Hansson, who owned Hanssonborg, the large estate where Erik lived. Erik was the son of a poor tenant farmer, but Greta had always treated him like her own little brother. They were often together, and Erik thought her as beautiful as any fairy-tale princess.

"Carried off the lovely princess,

To his gloomy dungeon— "

Suddenly Erik stopped singing and stood still to listen. He had heard the music of sleigh bells on the other side of the snowy pine forest. Now came the thud of horses' hoofs and the crunch of a sleigh's runners, as it stopped before the Hansson home.

"Christmas is coming!" smiled Erik, and struck out again in big, vigorous strides. Christmas in Sweden means visitors and fun and lots of food; and Erik licked his lips. His cheeks glowed with health like ruddy, round apples. His blue eyes caught the icy sparkles from under his feet, and he began to sing once more.

"So the brave prince slew the giant,

Carried off the princess fair."

But Erik would not have been so happy if he had known who it was that had just arrived at Hanssonborg. He would not have sung so lustily about wicked giants carrying off fair princesses. For something unpleasant and very real was happening to his friend Greta.

Darkness was falling fast. In Sweden, the winter sunlight is shy. It shows itself late in the morning, and then by early afternoon, it has run away again.

Erik skated to shore. He took off his skates and started walking through the woods toward home. A Swedish law says that everyone who cuts down a tree must plant a new one; so the Swedish forests are thick and beautiful.

Little, lighted candles glowed in the windows of Erik's cottage, which was painted red and had white window frames. Vacation time was a good time, he thought, as he stamped into the cozy kitchen, where a big fire crackled.

His brother Nils sat at a rough, wooden table. Nils's arms were crossed in front of him, and his head rested upon them. How could he study with his head so low? Surely he was not asleep—not big Nils! Why, he was always far too busy studying his farm books or working on the estate to fall asleep in the daytime. What was the matter?

Erik stood in the center of the room with his legs apart and his snow cap pushed back upon his fair, curly hair.

"Ho, Nils!" he shouted.

The older brother did not stir. Erik went over and tapped him on the shoulder.

"I say, what's wrong?"

The young man raised his head. He had a strong, brave face, but just now there was a shadow over it.

"Have you heard the news?" he asked.

The little boy shook his head.

"Baron Karl von Engstrom from Stockholm arrived at Hanssonborg today," said Nils. "He is to spend the holidays here, and they say that he will ask Fru Hansson for Greta's hand in marriage."

Erik's mouth fell open. His eyes widened with horror. A baron from Stockholm! Greta's hand in marriage!

The memory of a few lines from his fairy-tale book flashed over him:

"Down the mountainside came thundering,

Fierce and wild, a giant tall,

Carried off the lovely princess—"

"No, no, Nils," cried Erik. "You can't let him do it. You shan't!"

Nils smiled, but it was a bitter smile. "What are you saying?" he asked Erik. "Do you think that I, a poor tenant farmer, could possibly prevent the marriage of Fru Hansson's daughter?"

"Yes, yes!" screamed Erik. "You must! You shan't allow this giant—this Baron to marry her!" He recalled the words of his song,

"Then the brave prince slew the giant,

Carried off the princess fair."

And he added, "You must march against him. That's what you must do. With a sword and—and a shield and—"

"And if you don't watch out, you'll drop that platter," laughed Nils.

Erik put down the platter and the knife. He had snatched them up in his anger and excitement, to use them as a shield and a sword.

Oh, but Greta must never marry anybody but Nils! Ever since childhood, they had been the best of friends, and Erik knew that his big brother loved Greta dearly.

However, he had never told her so, for Fru Hansson was proud and belonged to an old, aristocratic family, while Nils was only a peasant. Still in thefairy tales it was always poor Boots who won the princess in the end, because he was brave and cut off the heads of giants.

At the supper table, Erik, who usually did all the talking, was strangely quiet. He did not ask for second helpings of food—which worried his mother. And when, soon after supper, he stole silently away to bed, she decided that all was not well.

When she came to kiss him good night in his funny little cupboard bed built into the wall, she found him scowling to himself and mumbling.

"What's the matter, Erik?" she asked.

"Then off came his head!" answered Erik to the ceiling.

"Off came—what?" cried the astonished mother.

"His head. The giant's," said Erik. "It happened in a fairy tale. The prince slew him with his sword and rescued the princess and—"

"Go to sleep," said his mother, and tucked him in.

That night Erik dreamed of Baron Karl. He was a monster with long, hairy arms; with shoulders like huge boulders and a neck as thick as a bull's.

Next morning Erik could hardly wait to see this terrible creature—this enemy who had come to take Greta away from Nils. So he ran over to the big house and stood outside in the courtyard. He knew that soon the family would be coming out on their way to church. Sunday chimes already were ringing from the near-by village.

Hanssonborg had been built over two hundred years ago. "Borg" means "fort," and that is what it had been, like many other castles in Sweden. But today it looked tired and weatherbeaten.

Snow was falling and the wind whistled through the big chimneys. But Erik did not mind the cold. He was used to it. Besides, his ancestors had roamed icy wastes. Some may even have been brave Vikings—pirates who sailed the northern seas in high-prowed galleys. He was a sturdy boy.

Presently the front door opened, and Fru Hansson walked out. She was straight and tall. Next came Greta, like a lovely, slender flower, and beside her—No, no, it could not be true!

The Baron was far from a giant. Indeed, he was not much taller than Erik himself. Furthermore, he was thin and puny, and his pinched little face peered out through the folds of a great coat.

Erik thought of the wicked gnomes of legend who forged iron in their underground caverns. Some people believe these to be the iron mines of modern Sweden.

The Baron looked like a wizened little gnome.

Erik saw him shiver and draw his warm coat closer about him.

"I shall catch cold!" he muttered, and Erik clenched his strong young fists together.

"He's a weakling!" thought the boy miserably. "A weakling!"

Erik could imagine nothing worse.

CHAPTER II

THE GHOST

The longer Baron Karl von Engstrom remained at Hanssonborg, the less did Erik like him. In the first place, Greta now spent all her time with him; and that meant no more story or music hours with Erik.

Then, to Erik, a man without strength was like a meal without food. The men of his country were brave. Colonel Lindbergh's family came from Sweden. But Erik could not help feeling that the Baron was not only weak, but a coward. And at last something happened to show Erik that he was right.

One night after dinner, when the bright moon painted the snow silver, Erik watched Greta and Baron Karl come out of the house. They were followed by Greta's big dogs.

Every evening these dogs were given their last run and always by someone in the family. This duty was called "looking at the stars." And while Greta and Karl were "looking at the stars," Erik was looking at them.

The Baron was bundled up in his fur coat, but Greta had only a light wrap thrown over her evening gown. She ran off into the forest, the dogs barking at her heels. She thought, no doubt, that Baron Karl would follow her. But he stood there alone, shivering and scowling.

Erik hid behind a near-by tree. He heard the Baron mumble, "This is absurd! I shall freeze to death! The doctor says—"

Erik suddenly exploded with a loud "Boo!" and the Baron jumped up into the air.

He lifted his hands above his head and squeaked, "Help!" When Erik came out from behind the tree, he cried, "Don't—don't hurt me! I'm—I'm sick. The doctor says—"

However, when he observed that it was only a child who stood innocently smiling at him, he lowered his hands and stopped whimpering.

"Good evening, sir," said Erik.

Even though Erik could not help feeling contempt for this frightened little man, he was polite to Baron Karl. Swedish children are always polite to everyone. But he kept thinking of his brother Nils, who would not have been frightened by anything on earth.

Nils studied late every night, and that, Erik knew, was because he had a dream. He wanted to become the manager of Hanssonborg some day. He wanted to marry Greta.

There was no reason why Nils's dream should not come true—no reason at all. If only this cowardly little gnome of a Baron would go away! He must go away. And all at once Erik decided to see that he did.

The Swedes love peace. In fact, all Scandinavian peoples love peace. This fact is shown by the wise way in which Sweden and Norway, who were united for many years under a Swedish king, dissolved their union in 1905. Without the firing of a gun or the shedding of a drop of blood, the two countries broke the bond and settled their differences in a peace that has lasted to this day. For over a century, they have not had war, and Erik was as peaceful as a boy could be. But then, Sweden has never been invaded by a conquering enemy, and Hanssonborg had. Erik vowed to drive his enemy away.

A Swede by the name of Alfred Nobel (nṓ bĕl′) invented the famous Nobel Peace prize; but he also invented dynamite. Erik, who could sing like an angel, now declared war upon Baron von Engstrom. And the plan that flashed through his mind was like a flash of dynamite. What an uproar it was going to cause at Hanssonborg!

Mysteriously Erik looked about him, then turned to the Baron and asked, "Did you hear a sound, sir?"

The Baron had not heard anything.

"But I was sure I did," said Erik. "A ghostly sound."

The Baron gargled, "Ghostly? Absurd!"

"Oh, no, sir," said Erik seriously. "Hanssonborg is haunted."

Then Erik told him a legend which some of the peasants believed. The spirit of a warrior maiden was supposed to dwell in the walls of the old castle. Her battle cry was often heard at the dead of night.

"And that is why," continued Erik, as he watched the Baron's pasty face grow paler in the moonlight, "no one will marry Greta. For, you see, every time a suitor comes, he is driven away by these ghostly cries."

The Baron tried to utter a brave laugh, but it turned into a cracked cackle, like tin cans clinking together. Erik had an idea that the Baron's knees were clinking together, too.

"Absurd!" he repeated.

"Oh, no, it is not, sir," said Erik. He leaned closer and whispered, "It is a warning to those who try to win Greta from the one who loves her."

Before the Baron could answer, Erik heard Greta returning through the forest. So he called, "Good-bye," and ran off.

He was pleased with his plan. He had prepared his enemy for the ghost, and the ghost would cry tonight. He would see to that. Afterwards, he felt sure, the Baron would leave Hanssonborg forever.

He walked toward the back of the house. Erik's favorite room, whether in his mother's hut or in Fru Hansson's castle, was the kitchen. Especially at Christmas time, a Swedish kitchen was a joy to a boy's heart—or rather, to his stomach.

Ever since the middle of November, preparations had been going on—preparations which had to do with the salting and smoking of meat and the curing of fish.

"Good evening, Fru Svenson," said Erik, entering the kitchen and bowing low, while delightedly eying a platter of freshly baked buns.

The cook was his friend, and a very valuable one. She had the figure of a washtub, but her face was kind. She was drinking coffee at the kitchen table. Everybody is always drinking coffee in Sweden, whether it is in the kitchen or in the drawing-room.

"Will you have a spiced bun?" she asked Erik.

He answered, "tack," which means something like "thanks," and helped himself to two.

"Greedy little one!" laughed Fru Svenson. "Now you shall sing twice for me instead of once."

The cook loved music, and she never tired of hearing Erik's sweet voice. So when he had finished his two buns, he stood in the center of the huge room and began to sing.

This kitchen was a combination of the old and the new. Its cooking range had been built over an old oven. Modern electric lights gleamed upon ancient copper pots. In the pantry could be seen flat bread disks with holes in their centers, hanging upon poles from the ceiling. Everything was clean and neat. Everything shone.

Erik watched Fru Svenson's head nodding as he sang a soft little lullaby, and after he had sung another one, she was fast asleep. Now this was exactly what Erik wanted, and he tiptoed quietly out of the room.

Carefully he made his way through the big house that had once been a castle, through the hall, with its stone floor and whitewashed walls. A fire crackled in the grate. It threw weird light upon the suits of armor which glittered in the corners. They looked like live knights.

Erik hurried up the stairs and hid himself in an empty room. He waited there until the household was asleep, and then he crept out upon the roof.

Nearly every room had its own fireplace, and there were two huge chimneys. Erik knew Hanssonborg well. He knew which chimney led down into Baron Karl's bedroom. He began to sing into it.

He sang one of the wildest songs that has ever been written. It is called "The Cry of the Valkyries" (văl-kir´is) and it is from an opera, based upon a Norse myth.

The Valkyries were warrior maidens who guarded Valhalla (văl-hăl´a), the home of the gods. They rode through the sky crying, "Hoyotoho!"; and that is the song Erik now sang.

Greta had taught it to him, because Greta loved all the wonderful operas of Richard Wagner. She had seen and heard them performed at the Stockholm Opera House.

"Hoyotoho!" shrieked Erik in his shrill, boyish voice. "Hoyotoho!"

It must have sounded ghostly. When he thought that he had been a Valkyrie long enough, he stopped and let himself into the house again.

He hoped that nobody had heard him, except, of course, the Baron. The Baron could not have helped hearing him. But suppose Fru Hansson had been awakened and were to catch him as he made his way out of the house. That was a dreadful thought.

All at once, he heard a noise. Someone was up. Someone was after him. Had Erik been a Valkyrie, riding on the fleetest steed in all Valhalla, he could not have sped out of that house any faster than he did.

CHAPTER III

THE PLAN

Greta and her mother sat together in one of the downstairs sitting rooms. A fire burned in a fine old porcelain stove. Bright-colored, woven mats covered the wooden floor, which shone with a good scrubbing. Morning light filtered through the high windows.

Fru Hansson's white brows were drawn together in worried lines. She was deeply troubled. For though Fru Hansson lived in a castle, she was really poor. She was finding it more and more difficult to run her large estate.

Many of her neighbors had been forced to give up their lands because they could not afford to keep them. But Fru Hansson could not bear to think of giving up Hanssonborg.

That was why she hoped Baron Karl would ask Greta to marry him. Baron Karl was wealthy, and his money could save Hanssonborg.

It was not so much for her sake that she wished to keep it as for the sake of the tenants who lived on the land. They depended upon it for their living.

Greta was gazing out of the window. The oak trees in the courtyard were covered with snow. Their bare, black arms stuck out like chopsticks in a bowl of rice.

A knock sounded on the door. Fru Hansson said, "Come in," and the Baron came in. He wore heavy, warm clothing and had a muffler wrapped about his throat. He looked peevish.

"Good morning," said Fru Hansson. "I hope Baron Karl rested well."

The Baron frowned. "I did not rest at all," he replied. "Is breakfast ready?"

At the breakfast table, Greta watched the Baron's servant pour out his medicine. He took medicine before and after every meal, and Greta felt sorry for him. It was unpleasant to be ill.

Yet Greta could not help comparing the Baron to Nils, just as Erik had done last night. Nils was so very different—big and strong and fearless!

"The doctor says— " whined Karl's voice.

Always the doctor, thought Greta. He should marry a pill box or a bottle of castor oil!

"—I must have perfect quiet," continued Karl, "and so I'm afraid I shall have to leave Hanssonborg."

Fru Hansson gave a start. "But what has happened to Baron Karl?" she asked. "Has he been disturbed?"

The Baron balanced a herring on his fork and nervously blinked his watery eyes. "Yes," he answered. "In the middle of the night and by the most horrible noises!"

"Noises?" Fru Hansson looked astonished. "I heard nothing at all."

Neither had Greta; and the Baron began to wonder whether he had merely imagined those ghostly cries.

He coughed. "Er—well," he said, "it might have been the wind. Every sound upsets me so. The doctor says— "

"There was no wind last night," said Greta, and the Baron dropped a herring on the floor. One of the dogs gobbled it up.

The Baron's face turned red, but Fru Hansson laughed and said, "Ah, but Baron Karl really must stay—at least until after the Christmas celebration. I am sure there will be no more noises. Hanssonborg is extremely quiet."

The Baron toyed with a potato. He hesitated. Then he looked up and fastened his gaze upon Greta. Her hair was golden and her lovely eyes were as blue as Swedish lakes in summer. He did not want to go away from Hanssonborg and leave Greta.

"Very well," he said. "I shall stay. But if I should hear that horrible noise again, I shall leave, because the doctor says— "

The doctor again! Karl looked like a smacked pussycat. Greta speared a fried egg.

In the kitchen Fru Svenson told Erik what the butler had heard at the breakfast table. "So Fru Hansson persuaded the Baron to stay," she said, setting a pot of sausages on the stove. "And he will, too, unless he should be disturbed again."

"And what disturbed him, Fru Svenson?" asked Erik, his eyes upon the pot.

"A terrible racket in the night, it seems," she replied. "Though what it could have been I'm sure I can't imagine."

"A ghost, perhaps, Fru Svenson?" asked Erik innocently, moving closer to the stove.

"Certainly not," she scoffed, "because there are no ghosts. And take your hands out of that pot."

Erik, full of sausages, returned to his cottage on the edge of the forest, his mind full of a new plan. If the Baron intended to remain at Hanssonborg unless he heard the ghost again, well, then he should certainly hear it.

Erik would repeat his song, and that would put the final scare into the Baron. Hanssonborg would then be rid of him forever.

Christmas Eve would be a good time, thought Erik. On Christmas Eve the peasants were invited to the big house. Erik would slip away from the crowd of children and conceal himself in the house as he had done before. When all was still, he would become a Valkyrie and cry down the chimney.

He had his scheme nicely laid out. But there is a poem about "the best-laid schemes of mice and men" often going wrong; and Erik's went wrong.

This is how it happened. Upon St. Lucy's Day, according to the custom, a little girl awakened the household at an early hour. She wore a white nightgown and a wreath with seven candles in it round her head. She served coffee and buns.

She was one of Fru Hansson's guests and came from Falun (fä´lûn) in the province of Dalecarlia (dä´lĕ-kär´lia). Her father was head of a big factory, for Falun is an important factory town, in which is located the oldest copper mining company in the world.

The little girl was sweet and pretty, but when she sang, it sounded like a shrill whistle in one of her father's factories. Greta thought of Erik and of how beautifully he could sing.

Greta was proud of Erik. She had taught him all he knew. So that afternoon she asked him to sing for the guests on Christmas Eve.

Erik was shocked. This was going to spoil his whole plan, because if he sang in the drawing-room after dinner, the Baron might recognize his voice. Then he would not be frightened any more by the ghost.

"But I—I had expected to sing on Christmas Eve," stammered Erik, and Greta looked astonished. So he quickly added, "No, no, not to entertain the guests, but—" Then under his breath he mumbled, "To drive one of them away!"

Greta laughed and mussed his hair. But a sad, little thought showed on her face in spite of the laugh, and Erik knew that she wished the same thing, though she dared not say so.

However, something told Erik to keep silent about his plans. If she found out, Greta might think it her duty to stop him. She was really a grown-up, though he could sometimes forget it because she played so well.

He promised to sing for her guests. How could he refuse her? However, he decided that he would have to make his call to the roof of Hanssonborg before Christmas Eve.

The next days were very busy ones. More guests arrived. Everybody living on the estate received presents of pigs and cows and chickens. Even the animals, tame and wild, must have extra meals.

Erik assisted his father. Every day his mother went over to the big house to sew. She also helped to stir the Christmas porridge. It had to be stirred for ten hours, and several women took turns doing it.

Every night she would say to Erik, "Early to bed!"

She would see that he climbed into his little shelf, said his prayers, and went to sleep.

So he found it impossible to play ghost. And the Baron remained at Hanssonborg, with his nerves undisturbed and his mind almost made up to ask Greta to marry him.

As Christmas Eve approached, poor Erik grew more and more anxious. He must sing at the celebration. And what would happen to him if the Baron recognized his voice?

CHAPTER IV

THE CHRISTMAS CELEBRATION

It was the day before Christmas, and Erik was dressing for the evening's celebration. At noon, he had been to the big house for coffee with the other children from the estate. They had found high piles of Christmas presents in front of their plates, on top of each was a gingerbread goat called a "yule buck."

They had all had a happy time, unwrapping gifts and stripping the Christmas tree—that is, all except Erik. For poor Erik had not enjoyed himself at all. He had been thinking only of tonight and of his part in the evening's celebration.

What would happen to him if the Baron were to recognize his voice? Of course, if Baron Karl did not recognize it, Erik could still play ghost later on. He would hope for the best.

Yet as he, with his parents and Nils, made his way over to Hanssonborg at six o'clock that evening, his spirits were low.

All the guests met in the big kitchen, which was nicely decorated with ribbons and garlands. The first thing they did was to dip a huge piece of bread into the soup pot where the ham had been cooked. As each one dipped, he made a good wish.

Now the servants and peasants seated themselves around the table and were served by the family. The Christmas porridge took the place of soup and was eaten with sugar and cream.

Erik had no appetite—which meant that Erik was very much upset. He could not even eat the lutfisk (lo͞ot´fĭsk´) and rice pudding, though he was eager to know who would find the bean. The one who did was sure to be married before next year.

And it was Greta who found it. Erik saw the Baron smile at her, and he choked with such an explosion that his mother had to pat him on the back.

After dinner, everyone gathered in a large drawing-room. Here there was an immense Christmas tree with hundreds of candles on it. The gospel was read, Christmas carols were sung, and at last came the moment which Erik had been dreading.

Greta said, "And now, Erik, will you sing for us?"

She sat down at the piano and struck a chord. Her face was like the Christmas tree, Erik thought, only very much more beautiful.

As Erik sang, he kept one eye upon Baron Karl. The little man nervously wriggled his nose, something like a timid bunny. However, he did not seem startled by the sound of Erik's voice. It did not appear to bring him any unpleasant memories.

That, reasoned Erik to himself, was because "The Cry of the Valkyries" was so unlike the little folk song that he was now singing.

He began to pray that Greta would not ask him to sing "The Cry of the Valkyries." He knew how proud she was of his ability to learn such difficult grand opera. But oh, how he hoped she would forget it tonight!

He finished the folk song and bowed to the audience. They clapped with hearty approval.

The room was filled to overflowing. No matter how poor a family may be, at Christmas time a home is a home only if there are guests in it.

These guests had come from different provinces of Sweden. They were all very different, except in their love for and pride in their country.

The tall, fair man from Dalecarlia would have declared, in his singsong way, that his lovely, wooded province with its red log cottages was the very finest part of Sweden.

But the lady sitting beside him would have disagreed. For she came from picturesque Värmland (vĕrm´länd), a province of noted writers and inventors.

The short, dark-skinned man was a Lapp. He hailed from the icy northland, where the mountains are always wrapped in snow, where the sun goes to bed in the winter and does not get up for twelve long weeks. In summer, the sun refuses to go to bed at all, and for seven weeks the land is in constant sunlight.

It is the country of Santa Claus's reindeer, only in Lapland, the reindeer is Santa Claus. For it is meat and clothing and means of travel to these busy people, who are among the smallest in size and numbers on earth.

The Baron was chatting with a guest from Kiruna (chee rōōn´a'). They were discussing the iron mines of that province. Erik sighed with relief. The Baron had not recognized his voice.

Greta was talking with the wealthy banker who had arrived yesterday in a shiny automobile. He lived in the city of Stockholm, which is the capital of Sweden.

Greta was telling how she had taught Erik to sing, and how, too, she had often taught him his lessons when the heavy storms of winter had prevented him from going to school. They had become close friends.

The banker said, "The little boy has a beautiful voice. I should like to hear more of his singing."

Then he spoke of his love for music and of the fine operas he had heard at the Stockholm Opera House. And, all of a sudden, a chill shot through Erik, for the banker added, "Of all the operas, I like 'The Valkyrie' best."

He liked "The Valkyrie" best! Oh, now Greta would surely ask Erik to sing "The Cry of the Valkyries."

Erik started to tiptoe out of the room. If he could only disappear without being seen! He reached the door, and no one had noticed him. Just one more step, and he would be out of sight. His heart pounded; he cautiously lifted his foot, when, "Erik!" called Greta. "Come back!"

He returned to Greta's side.

"Herr Banker," she said, "wishes to hear you sing 'The Cry of the Valkyries.'"

Erik's stomach turned a somersault. He saw the Baron's watery eyes upon him. The guests had stopped talking and settled themselves for more entertainment. A fussy little lady from Hälsingland (hĕl´sĭng-länd), a province of rivers and forests, clapped her hands delightedly.

Erik began. "Hoyotoho! Hoyotoho!"

Suddenly the Baron stood up; his face was gray. Everyone turned to look at him.

"Hoyotoho! Hoyotoho!" Erik was shrieking as loudly as he could shriek.

"Hush, Erik!" Greta had stopped playing and had turned around.

The Baron shouted, "That is the voice! That is the voice I heard in the night."

Everyone now stared at Erik, but nobody except Greta and her mother knew what the Baron was talking about. Fru Hansson arose. In her proudly determined way, she walked over to where Erik stood beside the organ.

"Was it you, child, who sang at night and disturbed Baron von Engstrom?" she asked.

Erik's pleading glance sought Greta's face. But Greta appeared to be having a difficult time to keep from bursting into laughter. And what a dreadful thing that would have been! So she said nothing, and Erik answered, "Yes, Fru Hansson, it was."

"You see! You see!" cried the Baron shrilly. "I told you that I heard horrible noises, and I am never wrong. My nerves are so sensitive that the doctor says—"

"Why did you do this, Erik?" asked Fru Hansson. "You must have known that it was wrong to sing at such an unearthly hour of the night."

But now Greta came to Erik's rescue.

"The peasants," she said, "believe that Hanssonborg is haunted. Erik was playing ghost. It was only a boyish prank." She turned to Erik and laughed with a wicked sparkle in her blue eyes, "But you should have known, Erik, that intelligent people do not believe in ghosts."

The Baron said, "Glumph!" and sat down with a thud. Erik saw him pull a box out of his pocket and hurriedly swallow a pill.

Fru Hansson frowned severely. "You shall be punished, Erik," she said. "Such pranks are not amusing. Now go home to your parents, and tomorrow I shall speak to your father about this."

"Please, Fru Hansson!" It was the banker from Stockholm speaking. "Please forgive the child. After the pleasure he has given us here tonight with his singing, we should not be hard on him."

He turned to Erik. "Listen, my boy," he continued. "Will you promise me that you will never sing again to annoy people, but only to make them happy?"

"Yes, Herr Banker," murmured Erik.

"And will you also promise to sing again for me some day?" The banker smiled and put out his big hand.

Erik's small one slid into it. "Oh, yes, Herr Banker," he said, "with the greatest of pleasure."

As Erik made his way out of the room, he did not like the satisfied smile on the Baron's face.

Even less would he have liked the Baron's thoughts, had he been able to read them. For Baron Karl was telling himself that, since Hanssonborg was not haunted, there was no reason why he should not become its master. He determined then and there to ask Greta to marry him.

CHAPTER V

THE SPRING

Erik's family rose early on Christmas morning and went to church. On the way back, they stopped at the cottages along the way to drink with the peasants and to wish them a merry Christmas.

Erik stood at the window of his home as Greta and the Baron drove up in their open sleigh. They sat together bundled up in fur robes, and only the tip of the Baron's pointed nose showed. It was crimson.

As soon as they were inside the house, the Baron sneezed. Erik's mother had to fetch him hot water, and Erik's father had to heap the already blazing fire with more logs.

The Baron shivered and complained the whole time they were there. Erik saw Nils look at Greta, and when Greta caught his eye, she blushed. After they had left, Erik's thoughts were black.

For the next few weeks there was, Erik knew, no hope that the Baron would leave Hanssonborg. The days were full of jollity and feasting, and many visitors arrived.

Of course Erik could do nothing to hasten the Baron's departure. He had given his promise to Herr Banker that he would never again sing to annoy people.

Finally on January thirteenth, Christmas was "danced out," and the guests began to leave. Erik prayed that the Baron would be one of those to go. But each day he heard that the Baron had stayed on.

Vacation was over, and now Erik had to rise in the darkness of early morning in order to be on time at the village school.

SWEDISH SCHOOL CHILDREN PLAYING INDIANS

It was Saturday, which is the same as any other week day in Sweden. So Erik was skiing to school, when all at once he heard his name called and he looked around. There was Greta, skiing to meet him. As she approached, he saw that her face was pale, and it seemed to Erik that she had been crying.

"You are up early," he told her.

"I want to talk with you, Erik," she said. "We've not had a chance to be together for ever so long."

Why was she out alone this early in the morning? What had happened?

She answered his unspoken questions. "The Baron Karl has asked me to marry him, Erik."

Erik stopped so abruptly that he came near falling headlong. The color faded from his rosy cheeks, and his eyes became two wide, blue stars.

"But you will refuse!" he cried.

He thought of his brother Nils. He thought of the great sorrow that this was going to cause Nils. Then he thought of the Baron, who was a gnome and a weakling and must never be master of Hanssonborg.

"You will surely refuse him!" he repeated.

Greta smiled with a sad little twist of her mouth.

"Perhaps I cannot, little Erik," she replied.

As they continued on their way, she explained to Erik why she might be obliged to accept the Baron's offer of marriage. She explained to him that her mother was threatened with the loss of Hanssonborg.

"And we could never bear to give up our home," she finished simply.

Erik could well understand this. "Home," like many other words, came to the English language from the Swedish. The Swedes build homes, and not just houses. Their dwellings are not mere objects of brick and wood, but are living parts of themselves.

Perhaps this is because so much time must be spent indoors when the long winter months are mostly made of night.

No, Greta and her mother could never give up Hanssonborg. Yet, on the other hand, Greta must never be forced to marry the Baron. Something must be done.

Erik's head was in a whirl. That day at school he declared that six times nine was seventy. He answered his German teacher in French, his English teacher in German, and his French teacher in Swedish.

At bathing time, when the pupils had to scrub one another from head to foot, he poured a tub of water over his chum's head and nearly drowned the lad. Then he got soap in his own eyes and howled with pain.

There can be no nonsense about education in Sweden. Boys and girls are supposed to work seriously in school, and the result is that everyone in the country knows how to read and write.

So Erik was punished. He was given so much written homework that he decided to be careful of his behavior in the future.

The Baron left Hanssonborg at last. But Greta told Erik that he was coming back again. He would return in the spring, when he hoped that Greta would announce their engagement.

Usually the spring was awaited with eagerness. It marks the end of dark, bleak, wintry days. But Erik did not look forward to this particular spring. He almost dreaded it. For he could not forget that with the flowers and bird songs would also come the Baron.

Nevertheless, when Easter vacation arrived, Erik could not help welcoming it. He could not help being excited on St. Walpurgis (väl po͝or´gẽs) Eve, when fires were lighted on the hills and the young people sang.

At daybreak, Greta and Nils, with Erik half asleep on his shoulder, wandered toward home, happy and tired. They stopped at the big house, and Nils said, "Good-bye, Greta."

He touched her hand very gently, and she answered, "Good-bye, Nils."

Then she looked down at the earth where some tiny, sharp, green tulip leaves were pushing their way upward.

"Spring is here," she said, when suddenly Erik let out a piercing shriek.

"And the Baron is here, too!" he cried. "Just look."

Sure enough, Baron von Engstrom's elegant car was standing before the door of Hanssonborg.

From that time on, Erik saw little of Greta. But one day his mother sent him over to Hanssonborg on an errand, and he stopped to chat with Fru Svenson and to see what she was cooking.

He left the kitchen with a blouse full of cookies and the news that the Baron was ill in bed.

"What a very bad-tempered gentleman the Baron is!" Fru Svenson had exclaimed. "Always complaining and never satisfied!"

Returning home, Erik walked through the forest. A lark sang, and he stopped to answer. Snow still lay under the pines, but one felt the stirring restlessness beneath the earth, as of plants and roots asking to live.

At the shore of the lake, Nils was painting a rowboat and Greta was with him. Erik watched the sunbeams dancing on her golden hair as they danced upon the glistening water.

Greta was reading aloud to Nils. She was reading to him about the business of a market garden. It was the study that Nils liked best. She had often helped him with it before the Baron's arrival.

How happy they looked together, and how handsome, too! Like a god and a goddess in Norse mythology.

Erik approached. Greta closed the book and arose.

"I must go back to the house now," she said. "Will you walk a way with me, Erik?"

Nils stood up, too, and wiped his paint-smeared hands on his working overalls. He said nothing, but Erik could see the suffering in his face.

Oh, why didn't he tell Greta how much he longed to marry her? Erik felt sure that she would gladly give up the Baron for brave, strong Nils! Why was he such a fool?

Yet Erik realized that he was only a little boy; he could not know the ways of grown folks, so he was silent as he walked beside Greta.

She took his hand and squeezed it and he looked up into her face. She was crying. Then, all at once, she sank down upon a stump and hid her face in her arms.

"Oh, little Erik," she sobbed, "what shall I do?"

Erik put his hand on her shoulder and wondered what to say. It made him feel strange and small to have a grown person turn to him like this. It was almost as though he were the older of the two.

If he only were a man! He would be a banker and help Fru Hansson. He would give her as much money as she needed to save her home, and then Greta would not have to marry the Baron!

A banker! That reminded Erik of the Herr Banker who had visited Hanssonborg over Christmas. Why, he could help Fru Hansson. Erik suggested this to Greta, but she shook her head.

"Mother has already written to him," she said.

"What was his reply?" asked Erik eagerly.

"He refused," answered Greta. "Hanssonborg is already so heavily in debt that nobody will lend us any more money."

This was hard for Erik to understand. How could anybody refuse to help his beloved family? A strong bond existed between the landowner and the tenants, and to Erik, the Hanssons were like his own people.

"I will think of something," he told Greta, and reached into the depths of his pocket, frowning. "Have a cooky," he said.

In the weeks that followed, Greta stubbornly refused to permit the Baron to announce their engagement. Her mother pleaded with her and tried to point out the seriousness of their position.

But all Greta would say was, "Only give me a little more time."

Then something happened to Erik.

The school offered a trip to Stockholm to the pupils who could pay their way. These trips were occasionally conducted as a means of studying geography and history. Erik was delighted with the prospect of seeing the principal city of Sweden.

He was also delighted when he remembered that Herr Banker lived in Stockholm. Herr Banker had liked his voice and had shaken hands with him as if they had been friends and made Erik promise to sing for him again some day. An idea was already beginning to form in Erik's brain.

He raced home from school and counted his savings. He had enough money for the trip to Stockholm. Once there, he would call upon Herr Banker.

He decided to say nothing to Greta, however. He would keep his plans a secret until he could surprise her by returning home with the loan for Hanssonborg.

But he must see Nils at once. He went out into the fields to look for his brother, singing at the top of his voice. A cow stopped chewing to listen. A frisky little colt kicked up its heels and whinnied shrilly.

Greta was sitting in her mother's study. She raised her head when she heard Erik's voice across the fields.

"Happy little Erik," she sighed, and smiled through her tears.

Her mother said, "That does not answer my question, Greta. Will you tell Baron Karl that he may announce your engagement?"

Fru Hansson's desk was strewn with business papers. They had rows and rows of figures all over them. A photograph of the Baron stood above. It smirked down, as much as to say, "After I am master of Hanssonborg, you will not have to worry about these matters."

Greta looked at her mother's hands. They were thin and wrinkled. They were also white and delicate. They must never have to work.

"Please, Greta, give me your answer," repeated Fru Hansson pleadingly.

And Greta said, "Very well, mother. I'll tell Baron Karl today that he may announce our engagement."

CHAPTER VI

THE CAPITAL

Erik left for Stockholm. When he was gone, Greta missed him sadly. She missed his happy singing.

Now the only songs she heard were the Baron's laments and her mother's pleading, "When are you going to set your wedding date, Greta?"

To the Baron she replied as sympathetically as she could. To her mother she continued to answer, "Give me a little more time."

At last, however, both Fru Hansson and the Baron began to be annoyed. They wanted to send out wedding invitations. They could not understand why Greta kept delaying the wedding date. And poor Greta realized that she could not delay it much longer, that she must soon give in.

Erik, however, had not forgotten his decision to ask help of Herr Banker. He was, in fact, going that very evening to Herr Banker's home in Stockholm. But all day long, he and his schoolmates were busy sightseeing in the historic city.

A few wore the costumes of their province, which made a colorful picture as they tramped along the cobblestone streets. Stockholm is seven centuries old, yet her age has not made her in the least old-fashioned.

Her town hall is one of the most famous modern buildings in Europe. It stands with its copper head in the blue sky, and its feet in Lake Mälar (mâ´laṙ), bowing in the water to a reflection of the two-hundred-year-old royal palace.

Once during the day, Erik attempted to telephone Herr Banker. A telephone was a new and exciting experience to him. The operator said that she would get his number "in the wink of an eye," just as our operators might have said, "in a minute."

But Herr Banker was busy and could not talk with Erik. So, that evening, after asking his teacher's permission, he went to Herr Banker's home.

It was a clear, beautiful night. The twinkling lights of the town blinked into the many waterways. There were a hundred little islands, and the harbors were filled with ships that sailed to all ports of the world.

Some of them carried cargoes of silver birch logs—fuel for the city. The word, "Stockholm," means "Isle of the Log," but the "Isle of the Log" is built of granite.

At Herr Banker's home, the butler informed Erik that a large dinner party was taking place. Erik stood in the elaborate hall and heard the voices of guests from the dining room.

He could smell the delicious food and see a corner of the "sandwich table" (smörgasbord), which starts off every meal in Sweden. There were all kinds of cheeses and cold meats, breads, and delicacies of every variety.

The butler told him that it would be impossible for him to see Herr Banker now, but Erik begged to be announced. The butler scowled at him and disappeared. Erik hoped that the man would deliver his message.

Perhaps the butler would return and repeat that Herr Banker could not be disturbed. If so, he would have to leave Stockholm without seeing Herr Banker.

He must see Herr Banker tonight. It was important to Greta and to Fru Hansson and to Nils.

Off the hallway was a drawing-room. It adjoined the dining room. Erik tiptoed in.

On one side was a huge, stone fireplace. So huge was it that it might easily hide a person, especially a small boy. And when the butler returned, without having announced Erik to his master, there was no small boy in sight.

Crouched in his hiding place, Erik waited patiently. The dinner was long, but at last he heard the guests thanking their host and hostess, and he knew it was over.

The ladies filed into the drawing-room, and Erik held his breath with wonder at the beauty of their gowns and jewels. They were almost as lovely as the many flowers which decorated the room and which were delivered to the house as regularly as the groceries.

The gentlemen now entered. Herr Banker began to talk with an attractive, dark-haired lady, addressing her as Fru Minister Steinhardt.

In Sweden it is proper to use a person's full title, and this lady was the wife of the American ambassador. Erik's only knowledge of that vast country across the sea came through letters from his uncle, who had settled there.

He lived in a state called Minnesota. He wrote that it was almost as full of Swedes as Sweden. Half the farms were owned by Scandinavians, who had also had much to do with the building of a big American city called Minneapolis.

Herr Banker was laughing and joking and seemed in a good humor. But suddenly Erik wondered whether he would continue to be in a good humor if he knew that Erik was hiding in the fireplace. He might become very angry, and then he would not listen to Erik's plea.

A terrible fear came over Erik. What had he done?

Just then, Herr Banker announced that there was to be a musicale. He introduced the first entertainer. She was a singer.

As Erik listened to the clear, sweet voice, he forgot his fear. The melodies delighted him, and when the singer began a folk song which Greta had taught him, Erik began to sing with her.

Gradually, and unknown to himself, his voice rose higher. And so high did it finally rise, that at the end of the song, it was as loud as the singer's.

There was silence in the room. Everybody looked at the fireplace. Everybody's eyes puzzlingly searched for the unseen owner of that mysterious voice behind the fire screen.

Herr Banker said, "This is like a ghost story," and he walked over to the other side of the room. "Come out," he commanded, "whoever you are."

And Erik came out. He was covered with soot. He was black and mussed and soiled. He looked like a frightened little chimney sweep. He was on the verge of tears.

"What does this mean?" Herr Banker demanded. "What are you doing there, child?"

"Hiding," said Erik. His voice was choked. "I had to see you, Herr Banker. I had to! It was so important."

"You are the boy who promised never to sing again to annoy people. I remember you," said Herr Banker.

"Oh, I know, sir!" Erik's lips were trembling. "But when I heard the beautiful music, I could not help it. I forgot everything but the song."

Herr Banker put his hand on Erik's shoulder, and now he smiled. "Never mind," he said. "Perhaps, after all, my guests were not annoyed. Perhaps they even liked your singing!" He turned to the company. "Would you care to hear Erik sing again?"

Hearty applause answered this question.

So Erik sang. And, though his face was streaked with soot and tears, and his little costume sadly wrinkled, his audience seemed to forget it. Because his voice appeared to bring a great, light happiness to their hearts and to make their eyes see dimly.

When he had finished, it might have been noticed that several ladies took handkerchiefs out of handbags, while quite a few gentlemen were coughing. Yet none had colds.

Herr Banker told Erik to follow him into another room. When they were alone, he asked, "What is your name, child?" Erik wondered why his voice shook.

"It is Erik Lindgren," answered the boy.

"Erik Lindgren," repeated Herr Banker. "That name may some day be known to all the world."

He blew his nose. "Jenny Lind was a child like you," he continued, "and she lived in Sweden, too. One day she was heard singing a lullaby to her cat, and from that time on, a great opera house became her home. She grew up to be one of the best singers in all the world, and they called her 'the Swedish Nightingale.'"

Erik's eyes suddenly blazed with anger, and he threw back his head. "I am not a girl!" he cried. "I'm a boy and shall some day be a sea captain or—or a warrior!"

He looked very fierce, and Herr Banker laughed.

"No, no, Erik," he said. "Never a warrior! Ours is a peaceful land, remember. A sea captain, perhaps. But—" He sat down on the sofa and drew Erik toward him, saying, "Tell me why you came to see me, child. What can I do for you?"

He listened kindly as Erik told his story, ending, "And so, Herr Banker, will you lend Fru Hansson the money?"

Herr Banker was looking down at his hands. He was silent. The big hall clock ticked firmly, and Erik's heart pounded in time. What was Herr Banker going to say?

At last he raised his head. "You have asked something which is not easy to grant, Erik," he said. "Hanssonborg, like many other large estates, is burdened with debts. My bank has already loaned Fru Hansson sums of money. I am afraid we can lend no more."

"Oh, but, Herr Banker," cried Erik, "for Greta's sake! The Baron is a gnome!"

"The Baron is a—a gnome?" Herr Banker was puzzled.

"Yes, a sickly, cowardly old gnome!" declared Erik. "And Greta must not marry him. My brother Nils is strong and brave, and when he finishes his studies, he will manage Hanssonborg and marry Greta and pay you back your money—every cent!"

Erik drew a deep breath, and Herr Banker smiled.

"But where do you think I am to find this money to lend Fru Hansson?" he inquired. "That which is in the bank does not belong to me. It belongs to other people, who put it there to keep it safe. If I were to take it out and maybe lose it, I should be stealing. Shouldn't I?"

Erik had not thought of that. Nor did he know that his country was noted for its successful management of money affairs. The Bank of Sweden is the oldest bank in Europe. Erik only knew that he was bitterly disappointed and unhappy.

"So you cannot help Fru Hansson and Greta?" he asked, with piteous despair.

Herr Banker again blew his nose. It sounded like the blast of a trumpet.

"Come back again tomorrow, Erik," he said. "I will give you my answer then."

CHAPTER VII

THE WEDDING DATE

On the evening when Erik was visiting Herr Banker in Stockholm, Greta and Fru Hansson were sitting alone in their drawing-room at Hanssonborg. The Baron had gone to bed with a hot water bottle. He had sneezed twice after dinner.

The wind howled outside. It sounded like a pack of hungry wolves. Greta turned on the radio, but Fru Hansson made her switch it off.

She said, "You know that every sound disturbs the Baron."

Just then there came a terrific crash. Tiles were torn from the roof. The wind was trying to scalp the head of Hanssonborg.

"We cannot keep this house standing another winter without repairs," sighed Fru Hansson. Then she sat up straighter, and Greta could see the question forming on her lips. "When are you going to set your wedding day?"

Greta suddenly stood up. Her lovely face was flushed with anger.

"You cannot force me to marry a coward," she told her mother.

Fru Hansson stiffened. "But the Baron is not a coward," she said. "In his family are men of valor, as brave and strong as those in our own."

Greta laughed. "You surely do not call Baron Karl brave and strong!" she said scornfully.

"Perhaps not strong," replied her mother. "His health is poor—for which he is not to blame. But I am sure he is no coward. If he were, you know well that I would never ask you to marry him!"

Greta knew. She knew that Fru Hansson, fearless and proud, loathed cowards.

She started to walk back and forth in the room. Suppose she were to prove to her mother that Baron Karl really was a coward. In that case, she would not have to marry him. But what good would it do? They would only lose Hanssonborg. She was in a trap, with no way out.

Another blast of wind, and the whole house shook. One day it might fall down. They would have to watch it crumble before their very eyes.

Next morning, Baron Karl came down to breakfast in a sullen mood. He said that the storm had kept him awake all night. He told them that he would soon be leaving Hanssonborg. Fru Hansson sighed and gave her daughter a wistful look of appeal.

After breakfast, when Greta went for her usual stroll with the Baron, she said, "Please don't go away. We want you to stay."

Karl stopped and stared at her unbelievingly. It was the first time she had ever spoken to him like that.

"Then you will set our wedding day?" he asked her, and his nose twitched with excitement and hay fever.

"Yes," answered Greta. "Let it be whenever you wish it."

At that, the Baron became so excited that he swallowed three pills at once and choked. They had to hurry back to the house. Greta spent the rest of the morning weeping in her room.

Meanwhile, in the twisting streets of Stockholm, Erik and his schoolmates were again sightseeing. It was their last day. They were returning home that evening.

However, Erik was planning to go to Herr Banker's house that afternoon to hear Herr Banker's answer. He was seeing the city through a maze of worried hopes, praying that Herr Banker would agree to help the Hanssons.

Everywhere in Stockholm was water; everywhere were glistening waterways with ships upon them. There were bridges and harbors and quays.

The royal palace was the most important building. The teacher told them that Sweden is one of the few countries in Europe which still retains its king.

They visited the spot where, hundreds of years ago, the King of Denmark beheaded the leading citizens of Stockholm. This terrible tragedy is known as "the Blood Bath."

They stopped to admire a statue of Jenny Lind. Erik remembered what Herr Banker had said last evening about the "Swedish Nightingale." He had said that Erik, too, might grow up to be a singer.

"And I shall sing for Herr Banker all the rest of my life," thought Erik, "if only he will say, 'yes' to me this afternoon."

"What are you muttering about, Erik?" asked the teacher. "Why do you walk with your head in the clouds? You can see nothing that way."

It was true. Erik might as well have been in the moon. He had forgotten where he was, in thinking about Herr Banker.

Now he brought himself back to earth and found that they had arrived at the Outdoor Museum of Skansen. Old-fashioned cottages, tiny farms, and windmills had been brought here from every part of Sweden.

Children danced in the costumes of their provinces, and one could often tell to which parish they belonged by the dress they wore. If a woman was married, her cap was white. But if she was single, then it was red.

When the day's excursion was over, Erik started off to Herr Banker's. He promised to return to the hotel and join his schoolmates in time to take the train.

He ran almost all the way to the banker's house. Once an automobile came near hitting him, but he jumped upon one of the small safety islands. There he stayed for what seemed like weeks, while buses, taxicabs, motorcycles, and swarms of bicycles passed in a steady stream.

He would put down his foot and start to cross, when whiz!—something with an angry horn or bell would almost take off his nose. At last, however, he made a dash and found himself on the other side of the street.

When he reached Herr Banker's house, he rang the doorbell and felt his heart slide down into his boots. This time, the butler did not make him wait, but showed him right into Herr Banker's private study. There sat Herr Banker behind a big desk, smiling at him.

"Good day, Erik," he said.

"Good day, sir," gulped Erik and promptly fell over a footstool.

His face turned scarlet. He felt ashamed. He was only an awkward country boy.

"Sit down, Erik," said his host kindly.

Erik sat down upon the edge of a chair and leaned forward eagerly.

"Oh, sir," he breathed, "are you going to help Fru Hansson?"

The banker began, "I should like to, Erik, very much— "

"He's going to help! He's going to help!" sang Erik inside.

"But— " Herr Banker's smile faded and Erik's song died, "but I'm afraid that I cannot." There was a moment's silence before Herr Banker went on. "Still," he said, "I can do something else for you, Erik. I am planning a little journey through Sweden. I am taking my family along. How would you like to go with us?"

Erik's eyes grew big. He had never been on a real journey. This trip to Stockholm had been his very first. He had never traveled before in his whole life. He forgot Hanssonborg. He forgot Greta and Nils and everything except this promise of a new adventure. It was too wonderful to be true. He had always hoped to see the beauties of his country, about which he had read so much.

"Oh, thank you, sir!" he cried.

Then he remembered. Herr Banker was not going to lend Fru Hansson the money. Greta would have to marry the Baron, and the Baron would become master of Hanssonborg.

He rose from his chair. He twisted his little cap in his hands, and said slowly, "I'm sorry, sir, but I cannot go with you."

Herr Banker seemed astonished. "And why not, Erik?" he asked.

"Because," replied Erik, "I could not enjoy myself while at home there is so much sorrow."

Herr Banker stroked his chin. Then suddenly he clapped his hand down hard on the desk.

"Very well. You have won, Erik," he said. "I'll lend Fru Hansson the money. But it will be my own, and if I should lose it—" He frowned darkly, but Erik could tell that it was a make-believe frown. "If I should lose it, do you know what I'll make you do?"

Erik shook his head. He could not trust himself to speak. He thought that he might cry if he did, because he was so happy.

"I'll make you sing to me night and day forever afterwards."

Herr Banker laughed, and so did Erik, and it was all settled between them. Herr Banker was to secure the permission of Erik's parents and of his teacher, that he might go along on the trip through Sweden. Summer vacation would soon be here, so he would not miss school. Besides, the trip itself would be a wonderful education to the little country boy.

Herr Banker gave Erik a letter to Fru Hansson, written in his own handwriting. It promised Fru Hansson a loan on her estate, and Erik was to deliver the letter himself when he returned to Hanssonborg. What a glorious surprise for Fru Hansson and for Greta and for Nils!

But Erik did not know what had recently taken place at Hanssonborg. He did not know that Greta had at last agreed to let the Baron name their wedding day.

Fru Hansson was, on the contrary, delighted when she heard this. That same evening, they talked over plans for the wedding.

Greta was silent and finally the Baron said, "Greta has made no suggestions. I think she should be the one to set the happy day."

Greta wanted to cry out, "It will not be a happy day. I wish it would never come." But aloud she answered, "It makes no difference to me."

"Then let us be married on Midsummer Eve," said Baron Karl, and poor Greta felt a lump come into her throat.

Midsummer Eve is one of Sweden's most festive occasions, for then the sun is at its highest. Greta recalled the many happy times when she and Nils had danced around the Maypole with the peasants. For on that night, tenant and landlord celebrate together, and there is no difference in class.

Fru Hansson saw the tears come into Greta's eyes, and she quickly said, "Very well. It shall be as the Herr Baron wishes. The wedding shall take place on Midsummer Eve."

So the invitations were sent out.

CHAPTER VIII

THE TRIP

That evening Erik dined with the banker and his family. The banker's little girl was named Inga and the boy, Johan. Johan was Erik's age; Inga was younger.

When dinner was over, the children were excused from the table and both rushed up to their parents crying, "I first! I first!"

This same thing happened every day. They always argued as to which should be the first to kiss their parents and to thank them for their bountiful meal.

Erik was bursting with happiness and also with the bountiful meal. Herr Banker's letter was safely tucked away in his pocket. He wondered whether it might not be well to send it right off. But he decided not to.

He wanted to be there to watch Greta's joy and Nils's relief and the Baron's departure. Besides, what difference would a few days make? Erik could hardly have guessed.

And so, the letter still in his pocket, he left Stockholm several days later with Herr Banker and his family. They were bound for the island of Gotland.

As the boat pulled out of the harbor, Erik was so excited that he nearly fell over the rail. Johan pulled him back by the coattails.

Next morning at daybreak the passengers were on deck to see the famous skyline of Visby (vēs´bü), Gotland's "City of Ruins and Roses." It is one of the oldest in western Europe.

"They call Visby 'the Lost City,'" said Johan, "because once it was supposed to be down at the bottom of the sea."

Later as they entered the dream-like town, with its roofless ruins and rose-covered cottages, Erik almost believed the strange legend to be true.

But the truth is that, years ago, this tiny island town was the richest and most important trading center on the Baltic Sea.

Great walls surrounded it, with towers and gateways and moats. These walls are still there—a medieval memory of grandeur and strength.

The boys left Herr Banker, Fru Banker, and young Inga at an open-air cafe, sipping coffee, and started off to explore.

They stood in a market square before the ruins of a fine old cathedral, and they thought of the sacking of Visby. In 1361, the King of Denmark captured the town. He sat upon a throne in the market place, while the terrified people laid the wealth of their city at his feet.

There was a battle, and eighteen hundred peasants were killed. The boys visited a museum, where they saw relics and learned how the townspeople were tortured by the Danish king.

They felt further depressed, as they went to the spot where sea robbers of old were hanged. They gazed raptly upon the gallows tree where pirates used to dangle.

"Like washing hanging out to dry, I suppose," said Erik solemnly.

Finally they stood on the warm beach, and they thought of the Vikings. Johan told Erik that those rugged seafarers had once lived upon this island.

"They traveled to far countries," said the banker's son, "and they brought back their treasure. They settled in many other places, too: in Scotland and Ireland and even in North America."

Johan knew so much. Erik wanted to show that he, too, knew interesting things.

So he said, "Old Scandinavian legends say that Leif Ericson was the first Norseman to land in North America."

That was important. Erik stuck his hands firmly into his pockets and frowned knowingly.

But Johan added, "Leif Ericson was said to have named that country Vinland because he and his men found grapes growing wild there. Today it is part of the United States. Historians think it may have been the states of Virginia and Maryland."

Erik frowned more heavily than ever. Was there nothing that Johan didn't know?

Erik said furiously, "The Monitor was a famous United States battleship. It was built by a Swede."

"There now," he thought, "I've told him something."

But again Johan added, "His name was John Ericsson, and he also invented the first ship's screw propeller."

Erik made a noise like a porpoise coming out of the water for air. Could he never get ahead of Johan?

They started back to join the family. All the way, Johan talked about the disasters that had robbed Visby of her power: fights among the merchants, the Black Death, and the siege by the King of Denmark. Finally other countries captured her trade and Visby became "the Lost City."

The following day, the banker's party left the island and returned to the mainland.

"Little boys must never play with matches," said Herr Banker and laughed.

Erik did not know what he meant. They were on the train going to Jönköping (yûn´chû´pĭng).

When they arrived, Erik discovered that the town of Jönköping is the home of the Swedish Match Company. It was clean and well kept and full of flowers, though it is a factory center.

Erik wanted to see the factories, but Herr Banker informed him that it was against the rules for visitors to enter the buildings.

"They guard their secrets," said Herr Banker. Then he asked the boys some questions. "How many people on earth do you suppose use Swedish matches?" he inquired.

They looked at him with blank expressions.

Herr Banker answered, "Two out of every three. And how many different box labels do you think are made?" he next inquired.

Their faces resembled pink zeros.

"Nine thousand, and in different languages," he told them. "Certain uncivilized countries use these match boxes in place of money."

From Jönköping they traveled through the province of Smaland, (smō´länd) where for centuries men have been making glass.

In the south, they visited the Cathedral of Lund, where a sacred grove once grew. London, England, was also built upon a sacred "lund," which means "grove" in Swedish.

At noontime, people flocked to the great cathedral to hear and see a most unusual clock. Mechanical figures marched out, music played, and Erik's mouth fell open.

Inga, who was full of mischief, dropped her rubber ball into Erik's mouth, and he was so wrapped up in the music that he started to chew it. He came back to earth quite abruptly.

They were now in the province of Scania (skā´nĭ-a). The ancestors of these Scanians are supposed to have given the name, Scandinavia, to the countries of Sweden, Norway, Denmark, and Finland.

Scania is rich and beautiful. It is called "the granary of Sweden." Its plains are dotted with fine old castles and estates.

They reminded Erik of his beloved Hanssonborg, and he pulled the banker's letter to Fru Hansson out of his pocket. Should he send the letter to Fru Hansson?

Erik had gone out alone today and was wandering about the city of Hälsingborg (hĕl´sĭng-bŏr´y'). Johan had stayed at the hotel, nursing a blister on a travel-weary foot. Fru Banker and Inga were resting, and Herr Banker had gone to Copenhagen (kō´p'n-hā´gĕn), Denmark. He would be back for dinner.

Erik felt a bit concerned. The trip had taken much longer than he had expected, and there was, even now, no mention of their return home.

He stood on one of the many slopes of the city, which is called "Pearl of the Sound," and he looked across at the Danish coast. Over there was historic Elsinore, the scene of Shakespeare's play, "Hamlet."

Erik knew only one line from that play, and it was: "To be or not to be; that is the question." His question was: Should he or should he not post Fru Hansson's letter?

He did not want to post it. He wanted to bring it home himself. He could imagine the exciting scene. He saw himself handing the letter to Fru Hansson with a flourish. He pictured her beaming gratitude.

Greta would muss up his hair and laugh and call him her brave knight. Then the Baron would eat up all his pills, including the bottles, and Nils would marry Greta.

They would "live happily ever afterwards." These were Erik's favorite words in the fairy tales, and there was a whole library of fairy tales stuffed inside of Erik. He longed to take part in one.

So he decided not to post the letter, but to bring it home himself. It meant nothing to him that Midsummer Eve was fast approaching.

The banker's family journeyed to Gothenburg (gŏt´ĕn-bûrg), Sweden's second city and most important seaport. Herr Banker told them how it had been founded.

"One day," said he, "a little bird fell at the feet of the soldier-king, Gustavus Adolphus. It had been pursued by an eagle. Gustavus believed this to be a good sign, so he built a city in the valley below."

In the Gothenburg Art Museum they saw the paintings of Sweden's great artist, Anders Zorn. Herr Banker took them to the busy harbor. It was filled with fishing boats and many tiny islands, which looked like red-brown freckles on the water. The sun shone down with real Swedish energy, as though enjoying its work.

Erik heard Herr Banker say that tomorrow they were to leave for Stockholm. They were to cross Sweden in the train.

"And tomorrow night we shall be at home once more," said Fru Banker.

"Oh, let us go by way of the Göta (yû´tä) Canal!" begged Johan. "Erik has never been there, and it is so much fun!"

"But it will take three days longer," objected Fru Banker.

She was eager to return, for there was much to be done in preparation for the yearly holiday at their country home.

"Oh, please!" urged Johan, and now Inga and Erik joined in the chorus. "Please, please!" they cried. "The Göta Canal!"

Fru Banker hesitated. "The time is flying by," she said. "Midsummer Eve will soon be— "

But the chorus of voices shouting, "Please! Please!" drowned out her words.

CHAPTER IX

THE GÖTA CANAL

Fru Banker agreed to return to Stockholm by way of the Göta Canal. Herr Banker assured her that they would be home two days before Midsummer Eve; and so she was satisfied.

The attractive little canal boat pulled out of Gothenburg's cobbled docks. The Göta River made a lazy pathway through fields and meadows.

It was like floating through land, and one could almost touch the horses and cows in the pastures close by.

Erik felt just the way he did at the circus. There was so much to see that he could not possibly see it all. The river was so narrow in places that at times it seemed as though the ship would stick between shores. But the captain always steered them through safely.

The boat was lifted up and down for seventy-two locks. Erik never tired of watching the lock gates opening and closing.

Frequently the boat would stop to take on passengers and freight. At these times, Erik and Johan would jump off and wander about the countryside. It was upon one of these excursions that something happened to them.

They had been passing medieval castles along the route. Among them was Bohus, once a powerful stronghold, whose two ruined towers are now called Father's Hat and Mother's Cap.

Another was Läcko (lĕck´ō) Castle, which sits upon Lake Väner (vĕ´nẽr), the largest lake in Europe, except for those in Russia. Erik was charmed with Läcko's fierce mystery.

But as the great bulk of Vadstena (vaud´stān-ȧ) Castle came into view across Lake Vätter (vĕt´tẽr), Erik felt a thrill of pride. He could hardly wait to visit it.

Whenever the boys left the boat, Fru Banker cautioned them to remember to return in time. For, should they be late, the boat would go off without them.

Now, however, as they examined Vadstena Castle, with its ancient moats and ramparts, they forgot this advice. Their minds were filled with pictures of the days when Sweden was at war, when Gustavus Vasa (gŭs tā´vŭs vä´sȧ), who built it, gained independence for the Swedish people.

Wandering farther and farther from the boat, the boys talked of their hero.

"I heard," said Erik, "that once Gustavus Vasa dressed himself as a peasant and went from village to village, trying to raise an army with which to fight the Danish King."

Johan gave him a look which plainly said, "Everybody knows that," and added, "He had to give up, though. He started to leave the country, hungry and discouraged, when the people of Dalecarlia sent ski-runners after him and brought him back."

"There is a ski competition every year," barked Erik, "and the ski-runners cover the same ground that Gustavus Vasa traveled that day!" He'd show Johan!

But Johan calmly returned, "I've been there. I've seen his statue at Mora, which is the finish of the race."

Erik glared. Then suddenly and for no reason, except that he had nothing more to say, he cried, "I'll race you!"

They ran off in the opposite direction from the river and their boat. Like two wild creatures, they dashed across a road, where bicycles, like metal flies in swarms, rang bells of fury at them. An old gentleman, carrying a basket on the handlebars of his bicycle, became so flustered that he wobbled from side to side and nearly toppled over.

The boys ran on. At last, breathless, they stopped. The race was a tie. They were now at the other end of the village and, all at once, they both remembered.

"The boat!" they gasped. Back they started, dizzy and tired, stumbling wearily. "It won't wait!"

Erik had sunk down on the side of the road, and Johan now collapsed beside him.

"We—can—t-take the next b-boat!" he puffed. "It leaves t-tomorrow and will get us to S-Stockholm a day later."

"That will be all right," said Erik. "We're in no hurry."

It was like an adventure to Erik, and he was enjoying it. He did not realize what a day later would mean. He did not realize that it would bring him to Stockholm only the day before Midsummer Eve, when Greta was to be married to the Baron.

After a while they felt refreshed, so they decided to return to the river bank and find out whether, by any chance, the boat had waited for them.

They hardly expected this; but it is exactly what had happened. Herr Banker had persuaded the captain to hold the boat.

Herr Banker had growled angrily, "Those young rascals have forgotten the time. It's fortunate that their heads are connected with their bodies, else they'd forget them, too, and leave them somewhere."

He was trying to cheer Fru Banker, but she was distressed and quite certain that the boys were at the bottom of the river.

At last the captain said that he could wait no longer. So Herr Banker, his wife, and Inga prepared to go ashore, when along came Erik and Johan. They were just in time to clamber on board as the boat pulled away.

Fru Banker was so glad to see them that she hugged them both and forgot to scold.

But Herr Banker said, "I am going to punish you. I had planned to take you to Uppsala (ŭp´sȧ-lȧ) with me for Midsummer Eve, but now I shall send Erik home as soon as we return to Stockholm."

Erik was disappointed. He had always wanted to see the famous Uppsala University, founded by Gustavus Vasa, five centuries ago.

Yet, in a way, he was glad that he was going home. This punishment of Herr Banker's would mean that he could spend Midsummer Eve with Greta and Nils. How happy they would be after he had given Herr Banker's letter to Fru Hansson!

But Johan pouted and whined, "Oh, please, father, take Erik and me to Uppsala for Midsummer Eve. Please, please!"

Johan seemed to be able to work miracles with that word, "please." Erik could see that Herr Banker was beginning to weaken.

CHAPTER X

THE RETURN

"Tomorrow is Midsummer Eve," sighed Nils.

The blue lake near Hanssonborg glistened as Nils rowed to shore. It was the first time in his life that Nils had not welcomed Midsummer Eve. This year he dreaded it.

He hated the air of festive excitement that hung about the big house. Yesterday he had passed Greta, walking with her dogs, and she had run from him, looking like a frightened child. Nils had wanted to tear out trees by their roots.

"Tomorrow is Midsummer Eve!"

He beached the rowboat and stalked back to his hut on the edge of the wood. He wondered what Erik was doing and where he was. He had missed his little brother. Still he was glad that the boy would not be here tomorrow for Greta's wedding.

Erik would be heartbroken. He might even attempt some mischief and try to break up the wedding. It would be just like Erik. Nils remembered the ghost of the Valkyrie at Christmas time.

But that same morning, Erik was walking quietly about through a peaceful university with Herr Banker and Johan. For Johan's magic "please" had won again. Herr Banker had forgiven the boys and had taken them to Uppsala. He had left his wife and Inga at home in Stockholm.

They were now standing before the Uppsala Cathedral, the largest church in Sweden, and Herr Banker was saying, "Gustavus Vasa is buried here. Also there is buried here the noted naturalist, Linnaeus (lĭ-nē´ŭs), who taught at the university for over thirty years."

They gazed up at the huge castle on its hill. Those brick walls recorded history and the boys listened while Herr Banker told them the story of Queen Christina.

"Christina was the daughter of Gustavus Adolphus," he said. "When she was eighteen years old, she became queen. Only she insisted upon taking the oath as King of Sweden. She ruled for ten years, a colorful and brilliant personality. But then came the dramatic day when Christina threw off her regal robes, tore off her crown, and renounced the throne forever."

Down the pink-tinted paths they walked to the town. At their hotel, a telegram awaited Herr Banker. He frowned at it.

Then he lifted his head and said to the boys, "I am called back to Stockholm on important business. We must leave at once."

"But, Father, you promised we might stay here for Midsummer Eve," objected Johan.

"That has become impossible," said Herr Banker.

"Then Erik shall return to Stockholm with us," cried the spoiled Johan.

"No," replied Herr Banker firmly. "Erik must go home. We are quite close to his province. We shall put him on the train, and he will reach Hanssonborg this afternoon."

Johan began to "please," and Erik wondered whether he would again persuade his father. Herr Banker hesitated. Then he turned to Erik and asked him if he would like to return to Stockholm with them, or whether he preferred going home.

Erik was about to reply that he wanted to go home, when Johan caught his arm and exclaimed, "Why, of course you want to come to Stockholm with me, Erik. Think of the fun we shall have!"

For a moment Erik was tempted. It would be interesting to spend a few more days in the glorious capital, "the Venice of the North." He also wanted to spend Midsummer Eve with Greta and Nils. What should he do?

"Erik will come with us, Father," decided Johan, when suddenly Erik decided otherwise.

"Thank you, Herr Banker," he said. "I have had a fine trip with you, but now I must go home."

Johan always got whatever he wanted. Well, thought Erik, this was one time when he should not. So, a short time later, Erik was alone on the clean little train, bound for his province.

When he arrived home, the first thing he did was to rush into his mother's arms. Hardly had he done this, however, than he wriggled free again and flew to the big house—Fru Hansson's house.

He ran right through the kitchen, past the cook, like a flash of lightning. Then he broke into the library, where he found Fru Hansson arranging flowers. She looked up, startled and displeased.

"What do you mean by bursting in like—?"

But she did not finish, for Erik whipped the banker's letter out of his pocket, flashed it under her nose, and cried, "Here it is, Fru Hansson! A letter from Herr Banker! And it promises money for Hanssonborg."

Fru Hansson read the letter. Then she looked down at the delighted face of the boy who stood before her, as important as a Swedish Paul Revere. His blond hair was tousled, and his cheeks were flushed with excitement. He was waiting for the glory that was to be his. But it did not come.

Fru Hansson said, "This is very kind of Herr Banker, and we can use the loan. It was also thoughtful of you, Erik, to bring the letter. Thank you. Now you must go. I am very busy."

He was dismissed. Nothing had happened as he had expected it to happen. Only "thank you" and a cold dismissal! A shadow fell over the golden page of Erik's fairy tale.

He took a step forward. "But, Fru Hansson—" he began.

"I said I was busy, Erik," she repeated. "There is much to be done before the wedding feast tomorrow."

The wedding feast! Erik's cheeks paled.

"Oh, but Fru Hansson," he cried, "there will be no wedding now."

Fru Hansson had a straight back, and her head was like a proud swan riding upon it.

"Go, Erik," she said. "And you may tell your mother to come. Cook needs her to help in the kitchen."

Erik reached for her hand. There were big tears in his eyes.

"Oh, please, Fru Hansson," he said, "don't make Greta marry Baron von Engstrom!"

Fru Hansson felt a strange little hurt down in her heart. She squeezed the small hand and replied kindly, "I have given the Baron my promise, child. Now go."

Erik found Greta in the garden. As he poured out his story, she listened sympathetically.

"But even though Hanssonborg does not need the Baron's money now," he finished, "your mother will not call off the wedding because she has given her promise."

"And so," said Greta, "Karl is to be master of Hanssonborg tomorrow!" Her lake-blue eyes had turned ocean-green.

"Oh, but he must not! He must never be master of Hanssonborg," cried Erik. "Baron von Engstrom is a coward!"

Greta gave Erik a strange, quick look. "If my mother believed that," she said, "the wedding would be called off at once."

"Then she must believe it," said Erik, "because it is true."

"How can you be so sure, Erik?" asked Greta. "Baron Karl is often quite ill. We must be fair to him."

"I will prove to Fru Hansson that he is a coward!" cried Erik.

Greta laughed. "Come for a walk with me, Erik," she said. "It may be our last one for a long time."

They started off through the beautiful forest together, and by dinner time Greta had not yet returned. Erik had come home. He was in his cottage, gazing innocently out of the window. Summer twilight hung over the land, silvery purple. It would linger far into the night.

Fru Hansson and the Baron waited at the big house, but still Greta did not arrive. Servants were sent to look for her. She was nowhere to be found. Evening wore on. Now everybody on the estate was searching for Greta, and the Baron was having a chill.

Greta had disappeared.

CHAPTER XI

THE RESCUE

The Baron was having a chill. Yet he could not remain indoors when everyone else was out searching for Greta. So he stepped timidly into the garden. He sniffed the fragrant air and glanced nervously about. The night was warm, but the Herr Baron was completely wrapped up in his great coat.

How unpleasant of Greta to disappear like this! And just when everything was all planned for the wedding and everyone was so happy! Greta must be found.

He took a step forward, and as he did so, a figure suddenly appeared out of the bushes. Herr Baron uttered a sound like a steam whistle with the croup and began to tremble.

"Good evening, sir," said a clear, young voice.

It was Erik. He had come over to the big house purposely to tell the Baron the story which he now began.

"Greta was left out on an island," he whispered dramatically. "Out in the middle of the lake."

The Baron attempted a laugh. It was a sad attempt. He shook his finger at Erik.

"You naughty b-boy!" he stuttered. "Once b-before you tried to f-frighten me. I d-do not believe you! R-run away!"

Erik did not run away. "I've told you the truth," he said. "Greta is on that island, and if you do not go for her, she'll stay there all night."

The Baron bit his lip. "If this is true," he said, "I must send someone for her at once."

Erik bowed and was silent. But the Baron seemed to sense in his silence the question, "Why does not Baron Karl go himself? Is he a coward?"

The little man drew himself up. "Where is the island?" he asked.

"Come," said Erik. "I will show you."

He led the way to the edge of the lake. The white night lit up the countryside and gave to it an elfin beauty. Erik pointed to a deserted strip of land far out in the center of the lake.

"That," he said, "is the island."

The Baron swallowed a pill. "Where is the boat?" he gulped. His voice still shook, but Erik began to wonder if perhaps Baron Karl was braver than he had supposed.

If so, this would be a good joke on Erik. For it was he who had left Greta on the island. They had rowed there together that afternoon, and soon after they had landed, Erik had quietly slipped away in the boat.

Greta had cried out to him to come back, but he had paid no attention to her and had rowed rapidly to shore. He had been carrying out a plan to prove that Baron Karl was a coward. But now, if the Baron should really rescue Greta, that plan would fail.

"Where is the boat?" the Baron repeated, and Erik was about to reply, when the most terrifying scream echoed from across the lake.

Erik gave a violent start. This was no part of his plan. Something real must have happened to Greta.

He turned to the Baron, but the Baron was gone. He was running away, toward home. Erik rushed after him.

"Come back!" he cried. He clutched at the Baron's coat. "Please come back! Now, you must save Greta. She is in real danger."

Baron Karl's teeth were chattering.

"L-let me go!" he quavered. "I'll bring help!"

He broke away and fled toward the big house. Erik was left standing alone, and out of the silence came another scream.

Erik felt like the boy in the tale who cried, "Wolf, wolf!" for fun, and then one day was really surrounded by wolves. His harmless trick had turned into a horrible disaster.

He was too small to think of going to Greta's aid all alone. Nils! He would go for Nils.

When he reached his father's cottage, he burst into the kitchen where Nils was studying with the lamp shining on his face. He cried, "Quick, Nils! Greta is in danger." And in less time than it would seem possible, they were hurrying toward the lake.

The screams had grown louder. Puffing and panting, Erik followed Nils into the rowboat. Nils picked up the oars. He pulled them with powerful arms, and the boat skimmed ahead.

Before they reached the island, however, Erik pointed and cried, "Look, Nils! There is someone in the water."

It was Greta. She was struggling to keep afloat, sinking, then rising to the top again. Nils tore off his coat. He dived into the water and soon was back in the boat again, with Greta in his arms.

"Row to shore, Erik," he said, and Erik picked up the oars.

He saw Nils wrap his coat about Greta's shoulders. He heard Nils asking Greta what had happened to her.

Greta looked at Erik as she replied, "Erik left me alone on the island. As night fell, I thought of my mother and how worried she would be. I found a leaky, old raft and tried to return on it. But it sank, and I should have sunk, too, if you had not come."

"Why did you do such a terrible thing, Erik?" Nils was glowering, and Erik saw the scolding in his eyes.

Erik answered, "I did it to prove that Baron Karl is a coward."

Whereupon Erik told them how the Baron had run away. Then he lifted up his head and began to sing, splashing the oars about in time to his singing:

"The sun upon the silver lake

Is shining like a wedding cake."

He did not look at Greta and Nils. He did not have to. He knew without looking that at last they were telling each other the truth. The "happily ever after" part of their story was coming true.

At the big house, Baron Karl was calling out the strongest and tallest servants to go with him to the island. He was fussing about in a panic, and Fru Hansson's nostrils were beginning to quiver with irritation.

Fru Hansson could not help wondering why the Baron had not gone to Greta's rescue himself. Instead, he had returned to the house with shaking knees and a green face, whimpering for help.

The band of sturdy servants was now assembled. The Baron placed himself at their head, announcing that he would lead the way, but cautioning them to stay close behind him.

Feeling brave, with this great army of muscle to protect him, he started away, prancing like a perky cockatoo. But hardly had he reached the front door when Greta, Nils, and Erik entered.

The Baron and his troop halted in amazement. The Baron's mouth fell open like a hungry baby bird's.

Greta ran into her mother's arms. She explained what had happened, while Erik added his bit to the story. He did it with enthusiasm, and the Baron gargled and gurgled and finally cried out that Erik was not telling the truth. He glared furiously at the two brothers and commanded Fru Hansson to "send away those common peasants!"

At that, Greta turned upon him. "Nils and Erik are my friends!" she flared angrily.

The Baron coughed. "Absurd!" he answered her. "And be good enough to remember that tomorrow you are to become Baroness von Engstrom!"

Now, after what Fru Hansson had seen of the Baron's behavior this evening, she was at last convinced that he was a coward.

So she lifted her haughty chin and announced in a firm voice, "There will be no wedding tomorrow. Baron von Engstrom is advised that I forbid my daughter to marry him."

Next day, Erik watched the Baron's car drive away from Hanssonborg. As soon as it was out of sight, he raced over to the kitchen and, to Fru Svenson's astonishment, danced a jig on the kitchen table.

Then he fell into the flour bin. He came out white as snow and, though Fru Svenson wanted to be cross with him, she had to laugh instead.

The months passed. Nils had begun to help Fru Hansson in the running of the estate. He was proving a clever manager. But he had not yet asked for Greta's hand in marriage.

With autumn came cleaning time. And what a cleaning it was! Everything scrubbed and polished and washed! There were harvest festivals, at which the peasants danced on the threshing floor.

Erik spent as much time as he could visiting Fru Svenson, sitting over bowls of small shellfish, pulling off the claws, and stuffing himself. For this was crawfish season in Sweden and crawfish decorated tables everywhere. They were even designed upon dishes and napkins and painted upon signs.

Autumn was also shooting season, and hunting parties were given at the country estates.

All during the winter, the peasants spun at their looms. Everybody was busy. Fru Hansson began to count profits.

Yet Nils and Greta still hesitated about asking the proud lady's consent to their marriage. They feared that she would refuse it. Nils was only a poor agricultural student.

One day Erik received a letter from Johan, the banker's son, inviting him again to visit the banker's family in Stockholm.

This time, the family did not travel and Erik learned to know Sweden's beautiful capital. He even went to the opera. A guest artist sang in a foreign language, but the other performers sang in Swedish.

This experience filled Erik with a great desire to become a singer some day. He sang constantly from that time on, unless he happened to be eating or sleeping.

When he returned to Hanssonborg, he was eager to hear whether Nils and Greta had yet obtained Fru Hansson's consent to their marriage.

It was again midsummer, and over the door of his parents' cottage hung branches of birch trees. This was a yearly custom which started with the ancient belief that the spirit of the tree will bless the house.

"Mother!" called Erik, running inside. There was no answer. He stood on the pine floor. It had been covered with fresh birch leaves.

He called again. "Nils!"

Still no answer. Nobody was home.

He went over to the big house, straight to the kitchen, and there he found things in a state of bustling excitement. Fru Svenson's face was flaming red. Something was going on—something very important.

"Good day, Fru Svenson," Erik greeted her. "Where is my mother?"

Fru Svenson turned with a bowl of cakes in her hand. "Your mother is helping the bride, and you must not bother her. Are you hungry, child?"

Now Fru Svenson knew that this last remark was unnecessary. Erik was always hungry.

So she was greatly surprised when he ignored her question and asked quickly, "Is Greta to be married?"

"Tomorrow," replied Fru Svenson, and set the dish of cakes before him on the table. "She is to wed a great nobleman."

With a sudden shove of his arm, Erik swept the dish off the table, and it crashed to the floor.

"What!" he cried. "She is not to marry Nils?"

Fru Svenson's two big hands settled upon her fleshy hips. She narrowed her eyes at the broken dish lying in pieces on the floor. Then she raised them to Erik's flushed face. He was breathing hard, and the look he gave her was pathetic. With an unexpected gesture, Fru Svenson swept him into her arms and hugged him close.

"Bless you, child!" she cried. "Don't look like that. It was your brother Nils whom I meant when I said that Greta was to marry a great nobleman.

Nils is the greatest nobleman in the land and will make Hanssonborg a strong and clever manager."

The following day, the golden sun awoke and seemed to know that this was to be his day.

The pagans who lived in ancient times used to worship the sun, and the Swedish celebration on Midsummer Eve is as joyous and natural as those festivities which took place many years ago.

Greta and Nils were married in the village, in a pretty little church with a fat, round dome.

A Maypole had been set up on the estate, and peasant and landlord, servant and master danced about it.

Yet this was not the month of May, for "Maj" (maī) means "green leaf" in Swedish.

The Maypole was wound with green leaves and on the top were blue and yellow flowers, the colors of the country.

Far into the weirdly lit night, the wedding guests danced and sang, and above all the voices sounded that of a little human nightingale—one who was too happy to go to bed.

THE END